HORSELAND

HarperCollins®, ☙*, and HarperEntertainment™ are trademarks of HarperCollins Publishers.

Horseland #1: Welcome to Horseland
Copyright © 2007 DIC Entertainment Corp.
Horseland property™ Horseland LCC
Printed in the United States of America.
For information address HarperCollins Children's Books, a division of HarperCollins Publishers,
1350 Avenue of the Americas, New York, NY 10019.
www.harpercollinschildrens.com
www.horseland.com

Library of Congress catalog card number: 2007924692
ISBN 978-0-06-134167-0

Typography by Sean Boggs
❖
First Edition

Welcome to Horseland

Adapted by
ANNIE AUERBACH

Based on the episode
"YOU CAN'T JUDGE A GIRL BY HER LIMO"

co-written by
PHIL HARNAGE AND **CARTER CROCKER**

HarperEntertainment
An Imprint of HarperCollinsPublishers

CHAPTER 1

In the middle of a beautiful countryside sits Horseland, a wonderful sprawling ranch. Riders who come to Horseland find exciting adventures in the surrounding mountains and acres of wild forest, creating great friendships along the way. With a large stable, a tack room, and best of all, an arena for training, Horseland is the greatest place around to board, groom, and show a horse.

No one knows all the ins and outs of

Horseland better than Shep, the wise Australian shepherd. A herding dog by breed and instinct, it's Shep's job to keep the horses in line, and make no mistake about it, he rules with an iron paw. Although the horses don't always like it, they obey him because no one wants Shep nipping at their heels! Besides, when Shep tells the horses to do something, he's usually right. Shep simply loves Horseland. After all, it is a place where all the animals can talk to each other—as long as the humans aren't listening!

On this particular sunny day, Shep sits with Teeny and Angora.

"This is one fine place to call home," Shep says.

"Yes, Shep," agrees Teeny, a sweet, young, potbellied pig. "This place is really great." With a pink ribbon on her tail and a curious disposition, Teeny is a playful pig. She runs around neighing and snorting, pretending she's a horse.

"Teeny, no one's *ever* going to mistake

2

you for a horse," says Angora with a sneer. Angora is a beautiful, fluffy cat, but she fancies herself better than the others. She's the cattiest cat you'll ever meet. "You look exactly like what you are," she tells the pig.

Shep shakes his head. "You can't always judge someone by what they look like, Angora," he points out. "Take Sarah, for

example. Remember when she first came to Horseland?"

Angora looks a little embarrassed. "Hmm . . . yes. Pity about that."

Shep smiles. "It just goes to show you: Don't be quick to judge."

The herding dog is right. He has seen it happen with both horses and humans. . . .

A hawk was perched high on a branch, its cry echoing throughout the hillside. It spread its wings and coasted through the air. A deer carefully walked to the water's edge, bent its head, and took a long drink. Suddenly its ears twitched. It raised its head in alarm, looking left and right, sensing something was wrong. A low, distant pounding was building. Before long, the pounding was

louder and stronger. The deer dashed off in a flash, disappearing into the underbrush.

As the pounding grew even louder, it became clear what the source was: Five galloping horses raced by leaving swirling clouds of leaves and dust in the air behind them. Each horse had a rider wearing a helmet—and a big grin.

Will Taggert led the charge on his horse, Jimber. Golden-colored with black streaks in his mane and tail, Jimber was a handsome palomino stallion.

Molly Washington urged along Calypso, her spotted Appaloosa horse. "Hey, Will! Where *is* this place?" the African-American girl shouted.

Will's cousin Bailey Handler sprinted forward on his horse, Aztec, a Kiger mustang. "Yeah, where are you taking us?" he asked.

Will looked over and smiled, his blond hair blown back by the wind. "Trust me," he replied. Although only fourteen years old,

Will was the most experienced rider in the group.

The horses splashed through a shallow mountain stream and then galloped through the trees. All the horses ran vigorously, excited to be out of the stable and on a new adven-

ture. Shep was along for the journey as well. He barked as he ran, keeping up with the horses.

Finally, the group came into a flat, grassy clearing high on the mountainside. The view of the valley below was spectacular.

"*Qué lindo!* How beautiful!" said Alma Rodriquez, admiring the breathtaking scenery. The twelve-year-old Hispanic girl

dismounted from Button, a skewbald pinto mare. She patted the horse's white mane.

"Told you it'd be worth it," said Will.

All the other kids dismounted and joined them at the picturesque point.

"You can see Horseland and the whole ranch," said Alma, pointing to the expansive property in the distance.

"It *is* beautiful, isn't it?" said Sarah, her eyes lighting up as she looked out at the view.

Sarah Whitney hadn't been at Horseland as long as the others, but she was still quite taken with it. She had been riding since she was five years old and took to it like a fish to water.

"How'd you ever find this place?" Sarah asked Will.

"Jimber and I stumbled upon it, a long time back," replied Will. "We come here

every once in a while." Jimber neighed in agreement.

At that moment, Sarah's horse, Scarlet, tensed up. She looked toward the forest. She began pawing at the ground and neighing. The black Arabian mare felt something was wrong. Although she was known to be high-strung, she was also fearless . . . and often right.

Sarah immediately went to her. "What's the matter, Scarlet?" she asked the nervous horse.

The horse looked toward the trees and neighed again.

"What's got you spooked?" Sarah asked. She scanned the forest, looking for anything out of the ordinary. But everything seemed to be fine. "I don't see anything. Probably just the wind, huh, girl?"

But Scarlet pawed the ground again.

Sarah became concerned. She knew Scarlet wouldn't be restless unless there was a reason. "I know we don't speak the same language, girl," she whispered in the horse's ear. "But I know you're telling me there's something wrong out there."

Meanwhile, the others were setting up the picnic lunch. Bailey pulled out a red-and-white-checked blanket and he and Alma spread it out on the grass. Molly grabbed the picnic basket and began unloading its contents. She put out delicious

sandwiches, crisp apples, some lemonade, and a yummy dessert for everyone to enjoy. Her mouth watered just looking at the food.

Bailey looked for his missing friend. "Why is Sarah taking so long with Scarlet?" he asked.

Alma giggled. "Sometimes I think Sarah speaks horse," she said. "She has a gift, you know."

When Sarah joined the group a few minutes later, Alma asked her what was going on.

"Something's bugging Scarlet," Sarah explained, still puzzled. "But I don't know what."

"Is she keeping secrets from you again?" Molly asked with a laugh. Likable and funny, she was always the first one to crack a joke.

Sarah shook her head and sat down. But she wasn't laughing; she was too concerned about Scarlet.

"Hey, don't feel bad, Sarah," Bailey said to her. "Nobody tells me anything either."

Will shook his head. "You guys shouldn't laugh. You know Sarah has a way with horses," he reminded the others.

"It's true," added Alma. "Remember that first day at Horseland?"

Molly and Bailey nodded as their smiles disappeared.

"Oh, come on, it wasn't a big deal," said Sarah, shyly, trying to dismiss it.

Everyone thought back to Sarah's arrival. It *was* a big deal.

"The first time we saw you, Sarah," began Alma, "it didn't start out very well. And it only got worse . . ."

CHAPTER 3

One bright, sunny morning not so long ago, Molly and Alma headed toward the stable. They were surprised to see so much activity going on at Horseland. Everyone seemed to be busy with a different job. Riders were raking and stacking hay, cleaning saddles, and even washing the outside of the stable.

"What's going on around here?" asked Molly.

"Didn't we just do all the grooming and cleaning?" Alma asked, her big brown eyes looking around.

Molly shrugged. "The good news is the arena's empty," she said. "Come on, let's do some practicing!" Any minute that Molly could spend in the saddle was pure heaven to her.

But Will cut their plans short.

"Not so fast," he said to the two girls. He handed each of them a rake. "You can help me clean up."

Molly and Alma were disappointed, and their faces showed it.

"Bailey's mom and dad want the place looking extra good today," explained Will. Bailey's parents owned Horseland, and when

they weren't around, their nephew Will was in charge.

"Why? What's so special about today?" asked Molly.

"A new girl's coming," Will said. "Now get busy raking."

Molly and Alma groaned. Their dream of squeezing in some practice time instantly vanished.

Angora the cat walked behind them and stretched. She was listening in, of course. She jumped up on the fence railing to hear the latest gossip—her favorite pastime.

Just before the girls began to rake, they ran into Bailey, who was holding a video camera.

"Hey, what's with the camera?" Alma asked him.

"Dad's idea—to shoot a video of the lessons, for the new girl," Bailey explained.

Alma and Molly looked at each with disbelief. No one at Horseland had ever received such special treatment before.

"Just who is this new girl—the president's daughter?" Molly said half-jokingly.

"Close enough," answered Bailey. "Heard of Sarah Whitney? Her dad is one of the richest guys in the whole state."

That was music to the ears of two of the other girls at Horseland: Chloe and Zoey

Stilton. The spoiled sisters were rich and competitive. They loved clothes and makeup—the more expensive the better. The sisters thought they were better than the other girls—and had no problem reminding them of this fact. The idea of another rich girl to hang out with was almost too exciting for

words. They ran up to Bailey.

"A rich girl?" asked Zoey, bubbling with excitement. "One of *the* Whitneys?"

"Yeah," replied Bailey. "Mom and Dad want us to be nice to her because this could be really good for Horseland. So you two had better behave yourselves."

Chloe and Zoey traded delighted smiles.

"Oh, we will!" said Chloe, her eyes lighting up.

"Hey, we *know* money," added Zoey confidently.

"Make yourselves useful and help clean up," Bailey said to them.

But Zoey and Chloe didn't hear him . . . or they chose not to. As the girls headed off toward the stable, they discussed how much fun it was going to be to have another rich girl at Horseland.

Bailey shook his head in dismay. *Those girls will never change*, he thought to himself.

"Great," said Molly as she rolled her eyes. "All we need is another girl like them."

Alma agreed. It was bad enough that they had to work so hard to clean up for the new girl, but to know that she was going to be a spoiled, rich kid just made everything seem worse.

CHAPTER 4

"**A**ngora, is this more of your catty gossip?" Calypso asked suspiciously.

The horses were alone in the stable, and Angora had just told them about the new girl's arrival. Shep and Teeny stood nearby, listening.

"Very funny," replied Angora. "I got it straight from the horse's mouth: 'Richest girl in the known universe,' that's what Bailey said."

Chloe's horse, Chili, peered over the half-door of his stall. He was a gray Dutch Warmblood stallion, with a white mane and tail. Chili had a reputation for being mean and spiteful. Next to him stood Pepper, Zoey's horse. She was a gray Dutch Warmblood mare. Together, they were very much like their owners, selfish and stuck-up.

Chili gave Pepper a very pleased look. "You know, this new horse is going to be a real thoroughbred," he said.

"With papers, of course," Pepper replied snootily. She flipped her gray-and-turquoise mane. "At last! Somebody we can talk to!"

"You can have all the papers in the world and it's not going to make you a better jumper," Button said from her stall.

Pepper just turned around and ignored her.

Later, when the horses were outside, they saw their riders hard at work, preparing for the new girl's arrival.

"I haven't seen so much elbow grease

around here in a dog's age," Shep said, his bright blue eyes taking it all in.

Teeny spun around and nodded her head in agreement.

"You'd think royalty was coming," said Button.

"What do you figure this new horse is going to be like?" asked Calypso.

Aztec shook out his blue-and-black mane and nodded with disgust toward Chili and Pepper. "Like them—a high-stepping snob," he said.

Angora smiled to herself, her tail swishing up and down. "Ooh! Sounds like the fur's going to fly, and I've got front row tickets!" she purred.

What *would* the new horse be like? No one knew, but one thing was certain—everyone couldn't wait to find out.

CHAPTER 5

The sun beat down overhead as Bailey, Molly, and Alma worked hard in the arena. First, they needed to rake the dirt and make it look smooth. It wasn't long before the three were filthy, covered from head to toe in dirt and dust . . . and really annoyed!

"I can't believe we're doing all this extra work because her dad's rich," muttered Molly. "My dad's a dentist, and no one cleans my stable."

28

Alma nodded in agreement. "My dad manages this place, but nobody does my work for me."

"Hey! My dad *owns* this place and I don't get any breaks either!" Bailey pointed out. He wiped his forehead with his shirtsleeve. He doubted this new girl was going to appreciate all that was being done for her arrival.

"Well, I don't mind doing our own chores, but why are we doing everyone else's?" asked Molly.

Alma looked around. "What happened to Chloe and Zoey? Shouldn't *they* be helping?" she asked.

Bailey shook his head, disgusted. "Aw, those two always disappear when there's dirty work to be done. They wouldn't want to soil their designer duds," he said with a smirk.

As soon as they were done raking, Bailey and the girls worked on setting up the jumps. They put up a few vertical ones,

29

which consisted of two or three poles stacked one above the other. Standards, or wooden stands, supported the poles. A lesson was scheduled for that afternoon.

"When the lessons are done, we ought to let the new girl take all this equipment down by herself," suggested Bailey.

"I'm all for that," said Molly.

Suddenly, they heard a car approaching.

"Sounds like the new arrival is here," said Will. The others joined him at the fence to take a closer look.

But this was not just any old car. It was a long, dark limousine. The kids couldn't believe their eyes.

"Check out that ride!" cried Molly.

"Whoa!" exclaimed Bailey. "That limo's bigger than a barn!"

"She's even richer than we imagined!" said Molly.

The limo continued on the dirt road, causing curls of dust to swirl in the air. It was hauling a very long, luxurious trailer.

Molly crossed her arms and shook her head. "That's too much car for one girl," she said with a sneer.

"She probably has her whole prep school in there," Bailey said bitterly.

"We are *so* outnumbered now," Molly added, thinking of how many rich girls would now be at Horseland.

Chloe and Zoey, on the other hand, could hardly contain their excitement.

"Zoey! Look at that limo. It's bigger than ours!" cried Chloe. She was so excited, she felt she might burst.

"I know, Chloe! The day just keeps getting better!" Zoey said with glee.

Tethered nearby, the horses were feeling very curious as well.

"Would you look at that?" said Calypso, eyeing the huge, black-and-red trailer.

"Pretty fancy trailer for one horse,"

Button declared.

Shep shook his head. "Look, just because the trailer's nice doesn't mean the horse is bad."

Chili and Pepper, like their owners, could barely contain their excitement as they gazed at the deluxe trailer.

"Finally! A horse worthy of our friendship!" Pepper said to Chili.

"How do I look?" asked Chili, hoping to make a good first impression.

Angora licked her paw and smoothed her fur. She also wanted to make a good first impression. "Well, at least things are getting interesting around here," she said.

Just then the limo came to a stop and a chauffeur got out. The new girl and the new horse had arrived!

CHAPTER 6

The chauffeur opened the door, and Sarah Whitney stepped out of the limousine. Tall and graceful, her blond hair fell all around her. She was dressed in an exquisite red riding jacket with black lapels and a red tie. Her white jodhpurs were tucked into expensive black leather boots. She held a riding crop in her hand. Behind the fence, all the kids craned their necks to get a better view of the new girl.

34

The horses looked on eagerly, too, as the wrangler opened the trailer's door and the new horse was led down the ramp. She was a purebred, black Arabian mare named Scarlet. Her black mane and tail were streaked with red, making her look regal and beautiful.

Aztec gave a whistle. "Wow! She's gorgeous!"

Button and Calypso weren't as enthusiastic, and Aztec sensed a hint of jealousy.

Angora smiled a sharp-toothed grin from her place on the fencepost. It sounded like trouble in paradise . . . and that sounded good to her.

Sarah walked over to her horse and ruffled her mane.

"Here we are, Scarlet. What do you think?" she asked, taking in their surroundings.

Scarlet neighed happily.

"I think we're going to like it here," Sarah whispered in the horse's ear.

Just then Chloe and Zoey ran over to greet Sarah. They began talking a mile a minute, overflowing with enthusiasm.

Chloe shook Sarah's hand. "Hi, I'm Chloe. Welcome!"

"And I'm Zoey," said her freckle-faced sister. "Double welcome."

"That's a sweet riding habit. That is classic vermillion," Chloe said to Sarah, referring to the specific red color of her jacket.

"Love your hair," gushed Zoey. "And your boots. I have those in brown."

"Are they a size six?" asked Chloe.

"*My* shoes are a size six!" said Zoey.

Sarah was a little taken aback by all the compliments and attention. "Oh . . . well . . . I'm Sarah," she said. "Thank you for all that. But I'm looking forward to meeting *everyone* here."

The others watched with interest as they leaned against the fence.

"Looks like they're hitting it off pretty well," Bailey said with a frown.

"What did you expect?" Molly grumbled. She assumed that all rich kids must be like Chloe and Zoey.

At that moment, Sarah headed over to them and introduced herself. But Molly,

Alma, and Bailey were not very polite as they mumbled their names. They acted distant and cold. They said hello, but in such a way that made Sarah feel unwelcome.

Luckily, Will stepped in and shook Sarah's hand. "I'm Will. Don't pay any attention to them," he said, motioning to Bailey and the girls.

Chloe and Zoey rushed over and grabbed Sarah by the arms.

"Come on, Sarah," said Chloe. "We'll get you settled."

"We'll show you where everything is," Zoey added, as she and her sister took Sarah and headed off toward the stable.

Once they were gone, Molly turned to Bailey. "You see that?" Then, in a voice imitating Sarah, she said, "Hi, I'm Sarah. My trailer's *so* Euro. My outfits are all designer."

Bailey smiled at his friend's joke. He wasn't expecting much from another spoiled, rich girl and planned to steer clear of her if he could.

An hour later, Bailey, Alma, and Molly each held a tray and stood in line inside the cafeteria. Bailey's stomach rumbled: All that hard work outside had built up quite an appetite!

At that moment, Sarah walked in and stood in line behind Alma. "Mmm . . . smells good," Sarah said, trying to strike up a conversation.

It worked! Alma turned around and started to warm up. She said, "The grilled cheese is the best." But then Alma caught herself. "Oh," she added, "but probably not as good as you're used to."

Sarah looked at her, confused. Just then, Chloe and Zoey came into the cafeteria and saw Sarah.

"Oh, Sarah. There you are!" said Chloe.

"What are you doing?" asked Zoey. "Come with us!"

The sisters briskly escorted Sarah to the front of the food line . . . much to the disapproval of the others.

"See that?" Bailey said, his brow furrowed in frustration. "She cut right in front of us!"

It was clear that Bailey, Alma, and Molly weren't going to warm up to the new girl anytime soon.

CHAPTER 7

In the stable, Scarlet stuck her head out of her stall and looked around expectantly. She was trying to think of a way to be sociable and make new friends. "So . . . you like it here at Horseland?" she asked the other horses.

"Yeah, sure," replied Calypso in a disinterested tone.

"You bet," Button said from her stall across the way.

"Why *wouldn't* we like it here?" asked Aztec defensively. He was known for being hotheaded, and it was pretty clear that he didn't trust this new horse. He figured if she arrived in such a fancy trailer that she must be just like Chili and Pepper.

"Oh! I didn't mean that," Scarlet said quickly. "I only meant—"

"Hey, Scarlet. Never mind those old nags," said Pepper as she introduced herself. She was in a stall on one side of the new Arabian mare.

"And I'm Chili," said Chili, from his stall on Scarlet's other side. "You can talk to us."

Scarlet looked back at Calypso, Aztec, and Button. But the three horses turned away.

"Talk to the tail," said Aztec with a snort, as he whipped around.

Scarlet sighed sadly. She didn't know what she had done or said to make them act so unkindly toward her.

Close by, Angora, Shep, and Teeny were

watching what was happening in the stable.

"Go Pepper! Go Chili! It's a catfight! Oh, yeah!" Angora sang, excitedly. She did a little dance atop the stack of hay bales she was on.

Teeny, however, was confused. "But why are our friends being so mean to that nice horse?" she wondered aloud.

"Because," began Shep, "they've already made up their minds about her." He shook his head with disappointment. "You know, sometimes people and horses can be as stubborn as mules!"

Meanwhile, Chili and Pepper were bringing Scarlet up to speed on how things worked at Horseland.

"Stick with us, and you'll fit in just fine," Chili told her.

"Right," said Pepper. "You don't want to hang out with them, if you know what I mean."

Scarlet was puzzled. "What do you mean?"

Pepper tossed her head, her mane flow-

ing to one side. "Isn't it obvious?" she said arrogantly. "We're better than they are. We have superior lineage, better pedigrees. We are the best of the best."

"Horses like us have to stay together," Chili said. He and Pepper didn't want to have anything to do with what he called the other "ordinary" horses.

Scarlet didn't like what she was hearing. "No, I don't think so. I choose my friends for who they *are*, not for their pedigree," she told them, shaking her head.

Chili and Pepper couldn't believe their ears. How dare this new horse not think the way they did!

Pepper gave Scarlet an icy stare.

"Whatever you say," Chili said coldly and turned the other way.

CHAPTER 8

Sarah entered the tackroom with her saddle and equipment. Along one wall were lockers, and along another were bridle racks and girths, the straps used to secure the saddle in place on the horse. Molly, Alma, and Bailey were already in there, cleaning their tack.

"Hi," said Sarah. "Do you guys know where I should put my things?"

"Any open spot's good," said Bailey,

gesturing with a sweep of his hand to the saddle racks that lined one wall. He immediately turned back to cleaning his saddle.

"Thanks," said Sarah, as she headed toward a vacant saddle rack. She started to unload her saddle and other tack in a spot next to Molly.

"Uh . . . but that one's not open," Molly told her.

"Oh, okay," said Sarah, surprised. She walked to a different rack. "How about this one?"

"There was a girl using it last summer, and, you know, she might come back," replied Alma with a shrug.

"Right, got it," said Sarah. She looked around, unsure where to go next.

Bailey pointed to the far end of the room—far away from them. "I think there's

49

something down there on the end."

Sarah nodded. "Yeah, I understand," she said quietly.

Alma, Molly, and Bailey quickly finished what they were doing and left, leaving Sarah all alone.

Sarah tried to keep a brave face. She took a few deep breaths and told herself not to cry. But it didn't work. The new girl plopped down on a bench and buried her face in her hands, crying. She just couldn't understand why they were so mean to her or what she had done wrong. She wondered if she'd ever fit in.

CHAPTER 9

Sarah decided to give it one more chance. She pulled herself together, walked out of the tackroom, and found Molly in the arena checking on the fences for that afternoon's lesson.

"Can I help you, Molly?" Sarah offered.

"It's okay," mumbled Molly. "This is my job."

"Oh," said Sarah with a sigh.

Just then Alma and Bailey entered the

arena. They began raking the ground.

"Maybe I can help, Alma," Sarah suggested. "Do you have another rake?"

"I can handle it," replied Alma.

"Bailey?" asked Sarah hopefully.

"I got it covered," he answered, continuing to work.

Sarah looked back and forth between them and took a deep breath. "Maybe we started out wrong," she began. "Can we try again?" she asked eagerly.

"Look, Sarah, we're all the same here," Alma said, as she continued raking.

"Nobody's better than anybody else," added Bailey in a critical tone.

Sarah suddenly felt extremely frustrated. "I don't get it. I never said I was!" Sarah exclaimed.

But the others ignored her and kept on working.

Finally, Sarah gave up. "Never mind," she said, feeling defeated. "I guess I just don't belong here."

As Sarah headed back to the tackroom, Chloe and Zoey ran into the arena.

"What happened to Sarah?" demanded Chloe. She narrowed her eyes. "What did you do to her? Where's she going?"

"She said something about leaving," Bailey said casually.

Alma nodded. "Maybe she decided Horseland's not for her."

Zoey and Chloe looked at each other and gasped.

"You're kidding, right?" said Chloe.

Molly simply shrugged.

Chloe couldn't believe it. "Horseland gets one decent girl, and you chase her away?" she said.

Bailey avoided Chloe's gaze because he knew she was right. His parents needed

more paying students to be able to keep Horseland open, and he knew they would be extremely angry if they ever found out how he and the others had treated Sarah.

"I can't believe you judged her without giving her a chance," Chloe accused. "That's like . . . like something *we'd* do!"

Bailey frowned and looked at Alma and Molly.

"Okay, *that's* scary," said Molly.

"Do you think we maybe . . . kind of . . . jumped to conclusions about her?" Alma asked.

Molly thought about how horrible they had been. "Maybe. She *did* try to help."

"Let's cut her some slack and see how it goes, okay?" suggested Bailey.

Molly and Alma nodded in agreement, and the three of them decided to give Sarah a chance.

CHAPTER 10

ater that afternoon, Will assembled everyone for a lesson inside the arena. Each rider wore a helmet and was on his or her saddled horse. A video camera on a tripod had been set up off to one side.

Sitting astride Jimber, Will addressed the group. "You've jumped before, so I'm not bothering with basics," he began. "Today, we work on form."

Jimber pranced in place, showing off a bit for the mares.

"When you get near the jump, follow the horse's lead," Will continued. "Move like the horse moves." He leaned forward

to illustrate his point. "Keep your back like the horse's and your heels down. And you're going to slide to the rear of the saddle. Okay, watch me."

Will nudged Jimber forward, and the horse cantered to the first fence. As Jimber began his jump, he thrust forward and upward with his hind legs. Meanwhile, Will leaned forward, his back matching Jimber's angle of flight. He kept his heels down and let himself slide back. He easily sailed over the fence.

The others clapped, and Will and Jimber returned to where they started.

"Who's first?" asked Will. "Alma?"

Alma nodded. "*No problemo,*" she replied.

But trouble was brewing. . . .

Chili leaned over to Pepper. "Let's get Scarlet in a little trouble," Chili said spitefully. He had tried to bring Scarlet to their

side against the other horses, but she had refused. Now it was payback time. "Watch this!"

Scarlet was standing near Button. Chili leaned in and nipped at Button's flank. Button reared back, neighing in pain.

Pepper shot Chili an angry look. "What are you doing?!"

Before Chili could answer, he and the other horses watched as Button took off in

a panic. Alma frantically pulled at the reins, but she couldn't stop the horse. Button's legs hit the rails of the first jump and she stumbled, throwing Alma forward out of the saddle. Then Button went down, too.

It was a disaster!

CHAPTER 11

The other kids sprung into action, quickly tethering their horses to the fence. They rushed over to Alma.

"You all right, Alma?" Will asked, concerned.

Alma was lying facedown, stunned. She lifted her head weakly. "I'm okay," she said with a groan. "How's Button? Is she hurt?"

"I'll take care of Button," Sarah offered. "You get the vet, Will."

Will nodded. "Bailey and Molly, you help Alma," he ordered.

"You got it!" said Bailey.

Sarah ran over to Button who was lying on her side. She kneeled down by the horse's front legs, which were bleeding a bit.

"Easy, girl, easy," Sarah said, in a comforting tone. "It's not too bad."

Button raised her head and tried to get up. Sarah gently pushed her back down.

"Stay, Button," she said. "Don't get up yet. It's just a little scrape."

Alma was also trying to get up, but felt a little wobbly. Bailey and Molly helped her sit up.

"Button! *Mia querida!*" cried Alma, straining to see how her mare was doing.

"It's okay," said Molly, trying to calm her down. "Sarah's calming her."

"We've got to get *you* taken care of, Alma," said Bailey. He and Molly kneeled down beside her.

Meanwhile, Sarah was taking good care of Button.

"It's going to be all right, Button," she whispered in the horse's ear, trying to keep her relaxed. "I'm here and you're going to be fine."

Then Sarah took off her expensive jacket and put it over Button's bleeding legs, tucking it around them.

"Look at that! How terrible!" said a voice. It was Chloe. She and her sister were watching nearby and couldn't believe their eyes.

"I know! What is that girl thinking?" asked Zoey. "She's going to ruin that designer jacket!"

But Sarah had a way with horses. Most of all, she knew they were much more important than any piece of clothing.

By the fence, Teeny was nervously running in circles.

"Poor Button!" the pig cried. "Shep, we've got to do something!"

"No, we don't," replied Shep. "The new girl's a natural. She's all Button needs."

"Maybe," said Angora. She jumped down from the fence rail to the ground. "But her horse is a beast! Why, not even *I* would do something like that!"

Shep looked at the cat with a confused expression. "What are you talking about, Angora?" he asked.

"Didn't you see?" replied Angora. "Scarlet bit Button!"

Shep looked surprised . . . and a bit doubtful. Was it possible?

At the same time, the horses were watching closely. They wondered if Button would be all right.

"Poor Button," said Calypso sadly. She and the other horses looked on with concern.

"Everything's going to be all right," said Scarlet. "Sarah will help her."

Aztec glared at Scarlet. "If it wasn't for you, she wouldn't need anybody's help!" he accused.

"What do you mean?" Scarlet replied, shocked. "I—I didn't do anything!"

"She's right, Aztec," said Calypso. "Scarlet had nothing to do with it. It was Chili. I saw him."

Aztec looked over at Chili and then turned back to Scarlet. *That makes more sense*, thought Aztec. *Maybe I misjudged Scarlet after all.*

The horses looked over at Sarah. She was stroking Button's head, and the horse's

65

breathing had calmed down. Button nuzzled her gratefully. The horses couldn't believe how calm Button appeared to be. Perhaps Sarah really knew what she was doing.

Meanwhile, two other horses were also discussing what had happened.

"I don't see why everyone's making such a big fuss over Button," Chili said with scorn. "She'll be fine."

"I agree," said Pepper. "You shouldn't have bitten her, but it's not like one of *us* got hurt."

There was only one question remaining: Would the humans learn the truth of what really happened?

CHAPTER 12

Molly finished putting a bandage on Alma's arm and helped her to her feet.

"There you go. Does that feel better?" Molly asked her. Luckily, Alma was going to be just fine.

"It's not me I'm worried about. Oh, *mi pobrecito*! My poor little one!" Alma said sadly, looking over at Button.

Button was still lying down, but Sarah

had not left the horse's side.

"I can take over now, Sarah," Will said, as he approached her and Button.

Sarah stroked Button's head. "It's okay. I don't mind," replied Sarah. She liked feeling useful, and Button had calmed down, which was the most important thing.

"Your riding clothes are ruined," said Will, kneeling down.

It was true. Her clothes were dusty and bloodstained.

Sarah shook her head dismissively. "Clothes can be replaced. Horses can't."

Just then, Chloe and Zoey walked up to them.

"We saw the whole thing!" declared Chloe, her hands on her hips. She pointed directly at Sarah. "It was *her* horse that did it."

"That high-strung Arabian!" added Zoey.

"Oh, really?" said Bailey, walking up to the girls holding the video camera. "Care for a little instant replay?" He rewound the tape and pushed Play. Everyone watched in

astonishment as Chili nipped at Button's flank.

Chloe spun around and glared at her horse. "Chili! How could you?" she said, confronting him. "This is so embarrassing!" Her face was as red as the hair on her head.

Chili lowered his head, feeling ashamed of what he had done.

An hour later, the local vet finished up his work and drove away. Button's legs had been bandaged, and she was expected to make a full recovery.

"Sarah, the vet said you did a great job," said Will, commending her.

Sarah looked down at the ground, suddenly shy. "I didn't do anything special," she replied quietly.

Alma walked up and put her arm around Sarah.

"That's not true!" Alma told her. "You

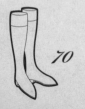

calmed Button down better than I could, and I've been riding her five years!"

Even Chloe and Zoey couldn't ignore the fact that Sarah had done a pretty heroic thing.

"Yeah, you did good, Sarah," Chloe mumbled reluctantly.

"Uh-uh," agreed Zoey. "I guess you have a real way with horses."

"Face it, *chica*," Alma said to Sarah. "You've got the magic touch. Thank you for saving my Button. *Gracias!*" She smiled and threw her arms around Sarah.

Molly and Bailey looked at each other with a grin. "Group hug!" they declared. They reached out for Will and all of them hugged Sarah. Even Button pushed his head in for a nuzzle.

"Count us out!" said Chloe, backing away from the group.

"Yuck!" said Zoey. "Let's get out of here before the mush gets any deeper. Come on." She and her sister turned and walked away.

Will and the others stepped back from

hugging Sarah. They were all dirty now, too, but they didn't care.

"I think somebody owes Sarah an apology," Will said, looking at the others.

Bailey, Alma, and Molly bowed their heads and nodded in agreement.

"Yeah," began Alma. "We thought you were going to be spoiled rotten and stuck-up, like Chloe and Zoey."

"But we were *wayyyy* wrong," Molly said. "Welcome to Horseland, Sarah."

Bailey suddenly looked worried. "You will stay, won't you?" he asked hesitantly.

Sarah broke into a beaming smile. "Sure!" she answered. She felt so relieved. Finally, she felt like she had been accepted by the group based on who she was—and not how much money she had. "I may be rich, but money can't buy friendship, and friendship is all I ever wanted," she told the others.

CHAPTER 13

The memory of Sarah's arrival at Horseland was one nobody would forget—whether they were a human or a horse (or a pig, dog, or cat!). Everyone was so glad that Sarah and Scarlet didn't leave that day.

On the mountainside, everyone was packing up after the picnic. Bailey, Molly, and Will put away the rest of the food and the picnic basket. Sarah shook out the blan-

ket and then folded it up. The horses were nearby, grazing on grass.

Suddenly, Scarlet's ears pricked up. She scanned the trees suspiciously. Her instinct told her something was wrong.

"What is it?" asked Aztec.

"Something's out there," replied Scarlet.

Shep sniffed the air. "I smell it, too," he said.

What was out there, and was it dangerous?

Will and Sarah approached Scarlet and looked in the direction the horse was looking.

"What's gotten into her, Sarah?" Will asked.

"I'm not sure," replied Sarah, worried. She put her hand on Scarlet's neck, rubbing softly. She wished Scarlet could speak English so she could figure out what was spooking her.

Scarlet whinnied softly but urgently, just as a growl echoed through the air.

Sarah quickly turned to Will. "I think we'd better get out of here—NOW!"

Just then Alma gasped. She pointed above the group. On a rock stood a menacing mountain lion, snarling and baring its teeth!

Will quickly grabbed onto Calypso's and Button's reins. But the other horses ran toward the lion in an effort to protect their owners.

The kids watched in shock as Scarlet, Jimber, Aztec, and Shep charged right toward the wild animal. Jimber reared up, and the mountain lion answered with a fierce growl. But the horses wouldn't back down. The big cat had no choice. Hopelessly outnumbered, it hissed angrily before turning tail and disappearing into the forest.

Scarlet, Jimber, Aztec, and Shep fearlessly ran through the forest after the lion. They wanted to make sure he wasn't going to make another appearance.

"Come back here, you guys!" called

Sarah, bravely running after the horses.

"Be careful, Sarah!" Molly called out. "The mountain lion may come back!"

Between the trees, Sarah was able to grab the horses' reins and lead them back to the picnic site. The horses neighed victoriously.

"Unbelievable!" said Molly when Sarah returned. It turned out that Scarlet was right after all!

"That was so cool!" exclaimed Bailey.

"Thanks for rounding up the horses, Sarah," said Will.

"That's our girl," said Molly, proudly.

"Sarah!" Alma suddenly cried. "You ruined your outfit again!"

Sarah looked down. Sure enough, she was covered in muck.

"Oh, well," Sarah said with a shrug. "They're just clothes." She knew that everyone's safety was more important than the latest fashions.

On the ride home, Molly and Alma rode next to Sarah.

"Sarah, you're nothing like what we expected," Molly told her.

"And we sure are glad!" added Alma with a laugh.

Sarah smiled. She was happy her new friends had realized it was bad to jump to conclusions about people.

At that moment, Bailey rode up between them. "Guess you can't judge a girl by her limo!" he said with a smile.

Everyone laughed.

CHAPTER 14

Shep, Angora, and Teeny watch the sun set from the entrance to Horseland.

"Sarah certainly did work out to be the best thing to happen to Horseland," Shep says. Although she was initially misjudged, everything had worked out in the end.

"Oh! Goody! Goody!" Teeny cries. "I'm so glad there was a happy ending!" She happily runs around in circles. "That was fun!

And we're all back to normal now. When's dinner?"

Perched on top of the Horseland sign, Angora rolls her eyes and sighs. Everything *is* back to normal, which in her book spells *b-o-r-i-n-g*. But with any luck, tomorrow will bring another unforgettable adventure to Horseland.

Sarah Whitney is a natural when it comes to horses. Sarah's horse, **Scarlet**, is a black Arabian mare.

Alma Rodriquez is confident and hard-working. Alma's horse, **Button**, is a skewbald pinto mare.

Molly Washington has a great sense of humor and doesn't take anything seriously—except her riding. Molly's horse, **Calypso**, is a spotted Appaloosa mare.

Chloe Stilton is often forceful and very competitive, even when it comes to her sister, Zoey. Chloe's horse, **Chili**, is a gray Dutch Warmblood stallion.

Zoey Stilton
is Chloe's sister. She's also very competitive and spoiled. Zoey's horse, **Pepper**, is a gray Dutch Warmblood mare.

Bailey Handler
likes to take chances. His parents own Horseland Ranch. Bailey's horse, **Aztec**, is a Kiger mustang.

Will Taggert is Bailey's cousin and has lived with the family since he was little. Because he's the oldest, Will is in charge when the adults aren't around. Will's horse, **Jimber**, is a palomino stallion.

Spotlight on Scarlet

Breed: Arabian

Physical characteristics:

- High-set, arched neck
- Short back
- Strong bones
- Outstanding stamina and endurance

Personality:

- Intelligent
- Spirited
- Strong
- Loyal

Fun facts:

- Arabians are the oldest breed of horse.
- They were originally used in the desert as a workhorse.
- Arabians have only 17 ribs (one fewer than other horses).

Sarah's Tack Tips

Tack is what we call our riding equipment, like saddles and bridles. Here are some helpful hints to make sure your tack stays in tip-top shape!

To clean your tack, you'll need:

- A bucket of clean, lukewarm water
- Two sponges
- Polishing cloth
- Saddle soap
- An old toothbrush
- Leather dressing

Tack Care:

- Clean your tack after every ride.
- Remove the dirt and grease with a warm, damp cloth. Scratch off the lumps of grease that build up, sometimes called "jockeys," with a blunt knife or coin. Then apply saddle soap with a damp sponge.
- Your saddle soap sponge should be damp, but not wet. It should not foam up.
- If you have synthetic tack, just wipe away any greasy areas with a damp cloth dipped in water and a drop of dishwashing liquid. Do not use saddle soap or oil on synthetic tack.
- Wash the bit off every time it's used. This will prevent it from accumulating dried saliva or food.
- Use a toothbrush to clean the hard-to-reach places on the girth straps, stirrup irons, and bits.
- Only put one saddle on a rack. Don't stack them.
- Hang up a bridle to clean it. It's easier!
- If you have to store your tack for a long period of time, wrap it in a pillowcase to keep it dry.
- If your leather tack gets wet, let it dry out naturally. Never put it near a fire or the leather will turn brittle and crack.